# Robotic
# T. Rex

By Paul Beck

*To Barnum Brown, without whom
it would be a whole different robot*

**Silver Dolphin Books**
An imprint of the Advantage Publishers Group
5880 Oberlin Drive, San Diego, CA 92121-4794
www.silverdolphinbooks.com

*Robotic T. Rex* is produced by becker&mayer!,
Bellevue, Washington.
www.beckermayer.com

If you have questions or comments about this product, send an e-mail to infobm@beckermayer.com.

ISBN 1-59223-210-8

Produced, manufactured, and assembled in China

1 2 3 4 5 10 09 08 07 06

06008

Edited by Ben Grossblatt
Art direction and design by J. Max Steinmetz
Illustrations by Davide Bonadonna, Roberto Campus, Roger Harris, Christian Kitzmüller, & J. Max Steinmetz
Product & toy design by Todd Rider & J. Max Steinmetz
Technical assembly illustrations by J. Max Steinmetz
Production management by Pirkko Terao & Katie Stephens
Cover photos by Keith Megay
Facts checked by Melody Moss
Special thanks to Megan Grimm for all her help with the Jurassic Chicken image

**Image credits**

Every effort has been made to correctly attribute all the material reproduced in this book. We will be happy to correct any errors in future editions.

**Pages 4–5:** Mecho-Gecko © 2003 Peter Menzel/menzelphoto.com, used with permission; Sprawl © Mark Cutkosky, Stanford University Biomimetic Robotics Lab, courtesy of Mark Cutkosky.
**Pages 16–17:** RoboBug © Danh Trinh/imaginerobots.com, courtesy of Danh Trinh; Scout II courtesy of Prof. Martin Buehler, McGill University; Honda Motor Company's Humano (ASIMO) © Reuters NewMedia Inc./Corbis, used with permission.
**Pages 18–19:** Cog © Sam Ogden/Photo Researchers, Inc., used with permission.
**Pages 20–21:** Robosaurus, www.robosaurus.com, courtesy of Mark Hays; Banryu © TMSUK/Sanyo; Jurassic Chicken sketch © 2003 Megan Grimm, courtesy of Megan Grimm.

# T. Rex Meets Robots

Ask anyone to name a dinosaur, and most of the time they'll say, "Tyrannosaurus rex." From fossil bones in museums to special-effects monsters in the movies, T. rex is probably the most well-known dinosaur of all. And no wonder! It's hard to forget an animal with teeth like six-inch steak knives.

Ask anyone to name a machine of the future, and you'll probably hear a lot about robots. Real robots have been around for more than half a century, but for most of us, a world where robots are common is still the world of the future.

Now the most famous dinosaur of the past meets a machine of the future in your robotic, walking T. rex!

## TABLE OF CONTENTS

# Robotic Copycats

When science fiction writers and others first came up with the idea of a machine that could do the work of a person, they thought it would look like a person. But when the first real, working robots were invented, they didn't look like people at all. Instead, they looked more like the bucket-lifting arms used by utility workers. Now, some scientists and engineers have come full circle. They're making robots that look and work like people and animals.

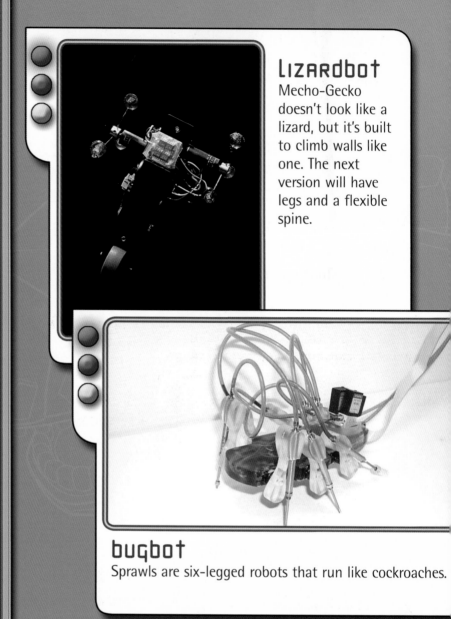

## Lizardbot
Mecho-Gecko doesn't look like a lizard, but it's built to climb walls like one. The next version will have legs and a flexible spine.

## bugbot
Sprawls are six-legged robots that run like cockroaches.

## Solving Problems Nature's Way

Robots have to be able to move around and interact with their environments. They do that in different ways depending on where they work. A robot with wheels would do fine on a sidewalk, but it couldn't roll over rocks. A robot with legs could walk around on rocks, but it would have a hard time swimming.

For robots, getting around can be a challenge. But for animals, it's a breeze! If nature has solved the problem of moving around in different environments, why not use those solutions in robots? Some scientists and engineers are doing just that. They invent new machines and materials by copying nature. It's a branch of science called *biomimetics* (by-oh-mih-MED-iks).

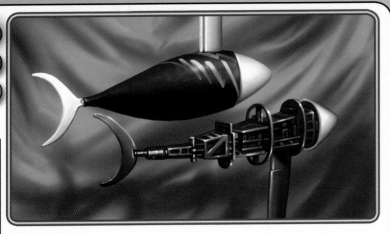

## fishbot

Charlie the RoboTuna was built to swim like a fish.

## to be a robot

A robot is a machine, but not just any machine. A robot is a machine that can:

- *use sensors to gather information about its surroundings.*

- *follow instructions, often in the form of a program.*

- *repeat itself, doing the same job over and over without getting tired or bored.*

- *work by itself or by remote control.*

- *move and handle objects.*

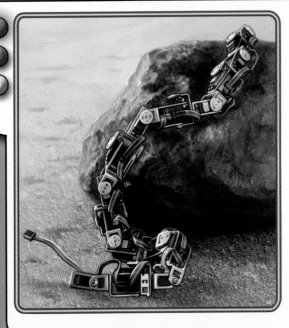

## snakebot

One day NASA's wriggling snakebots may explore the surfaces of other planets.

## Great Ideas from Nature

The shape and structure of water lilies inspired the design of the Crystal Palace at the 1851 World's Fair in London. The textured surface of a dog's pads led to nonskid deck shoes. The Eiffel Tower might never have been built if the designer hadn't noticed the inner structure of the human thighbone.

## The Ultimate Dinobot?

YOUR ROBOTIC T. REX WALKS LIKE A TYRANNOSAURUS. WHAT IF YOU WANTED TO CONSTRUCT A ROBOT THAT COULD DO EVERYTHING A T. REX COULD (EXCEPT MAYBE FOR THE MEAT-EATING PART)? YOUR FIRST STEP WOULD BE TO LOOK AT A REAL T. REX. YOU'LL FIND ONE ON THE NEXT PAGE.

# The Real T. Rex

If lots of big teeth make you the boss, then Tyrannosaurus rex really was the "tyrant lizard king" of the dinosaur age. T. rex ruled during the late Cretaceous period, between 85 and 65 million years ago. It was the biggest meat-eater of its time, and one of the three largest carnivores that ever lived.

5 ft.

### being king gives you a big head

T. rex's head was bigger than many people's bodies! The biggest T. rex fossil skull ever found is more than five feet long and three feet wide.

## The Better to Eat You With!

A T. rex's teeth were built for crushing bones and tearing off huge chunks of meat. The front and back edges of each tooth were serrated like steak knives, but the teeth were round, more like stakes than steak knives. The biggest fossil T. rex teeth are more than 12 inches long. Only part of each T. rex tooth stuck out from the gums. The rest was anchored in the jawbone.

## Gimme Four!

If a T. rex could count with its fingers, it wouldn't have gotten past four! Sharp claws probably helped T. rex hold on to its prey. The stubby forelegs were strong but couldn't move very far. The dinosaur couldn't even touch its own mouth!

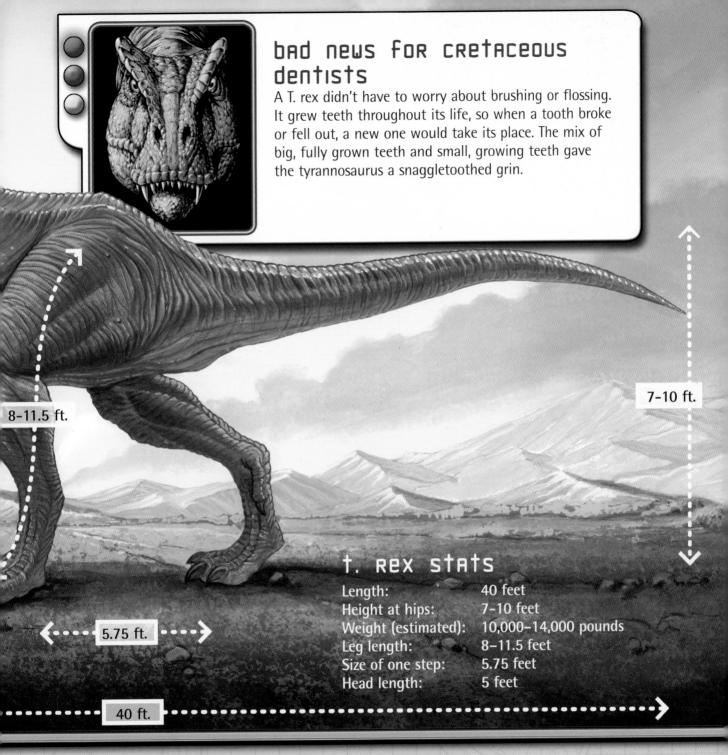

## bad news for cretaceous dentists

A T. rex didn't have to worry about brushing or flossing. It grew teeth throughout its life, so when a tooth broke or fell out, a new one would take its place. The mix of big, fully grown teeth and small, growing teeth gave the tyrannosaurus a snaggletoothed grin.

8–11.5 ft.

7–10 ft.

5.75 ft.

40 ft.

### t. rex stats

| | |
|---|---|
| Length: | 40 feet |
| Height at hips: | 7–10 feet |
| Weight (estimated): | 10,000–14,000 pounds |
| Leg length: | 8–11.5 feet |
| Size of one step: | 5.75 feet |
| Head length: | 5 feet |

## These Legs Were Made for Walking

A T. rex needed massive leg muscles to stand and walk. Even with such big muscles, walking speed may have been as fast as it could go.

## It's on the Tip of Your Toes

For such an enormous animal, T. rex left some pretty small footprints—about 18 inches long, only half as long as the tyrannosaurus's feet. Like all dinosaurs, T. rex walked on its toes. Animals that walk this way are called *digitigrade* (DID-jit-uh-grade), or "toe-walking." Humans and other flat-footed animals are called *plantigrade* (PLANT-uh-grade), or "sole-walking."

# The Ultimate
# Robo-Rex

*The ultimate biomimetic T. rex robot should be able to do most of the things a real T. rex could do. Here are some of the features it would need.*

## Super Smell

T. rex was a good smeller. There aren't any fossil T. rex brains, but scientists know from computer scans of fossil skulls that the parts of the tyrannosaurus brain that handled the sense of smell were really big!

## 3-D Vision

T. rex's eyes pointed forward in its head. This *binocular*, or two-eyed, vision let the tyrannosaurus see the world in 3-D. With binocular vision, each eye sees a slightly different view. The views get combined in the brain to give the animal (or you!) a three-dimensional picture of the world.

Machines can have binocular vision, too. Some robots use a pair of video cameras for 3-D vision. But there are other ways to take advantage of depth perception, or the ability to know how far away things are. Some robots use sonar (a system that "sees" objects by bouncing sound waves off of them). That's biomimetics from the world of bats and dolphins!

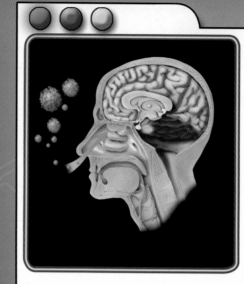

## your nose is a chemical detector

Smells are molecules of chemicals carried by the air. When the molecules come in contact with special nerve cells in your nose, the cells send a message to your brain and you recognize the smell. Some robots can "smell," too. They are used to find explosives, locate gas leaks, or detect poisons in the air.

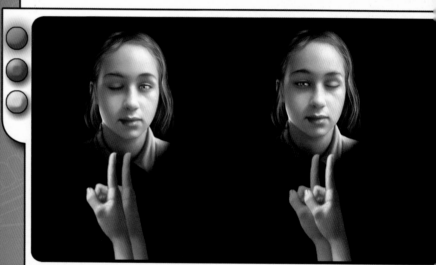

### binocular vision experiment

Hold up a finger about 12 inches in front of your face. Close one eye, then the other, and you'll see your finger jump back and forth. Each of your eyes has a different view. Depending on which of your eyes is dominant, your finger might "jump" in the other direction.

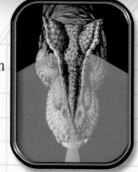

## A Tail for Balance

Balance is a big challenge for *bipedal*, or two-legged, robots. A tail would give a T. rex robot an advantage over humanoid robots, because it could help the dinobot keep from falling over on its face while walking.

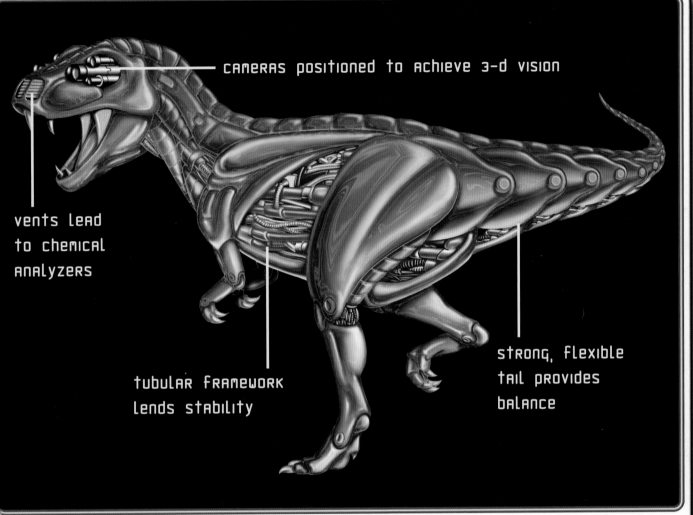

cameras positioned to achieve 3-d vision

vents lead
to chemical
analyzers

tubular framework
lends stability

strong, flexible
tail provides
balance

With the right equipment and engineering, a robotic T. rex could sense its environment and move around as well as its biological counterpart did.

## Inner Tubes

T. Rex needed strong bones to carry all that weight. Five, six, or seven tons is a lot to move. T. rex and other dinosaurs managed to do it with bones that were hollow. When you think about it, a T. rex skeleton was a system of bony tubes. If it's made of the right materials, a tube can be a very strong shape. At the same time, it's lightweight.

BIRDS HAVE HOLLOW BONES, TOO. MANY SCIENTISTS BELIEVE THAT BIRDS ARE THE MODERN-DAY DESCENDANTS OF DINOSAURS.

# How Do They Know?

*Wait a minute! We're talking about what a T. rex robot should do, but how does anyone know? There hasn't been a T. rex around for 65 million years!*

*Putting together a picture of T. rex is like doing detective work. Most T. rex detectives are known as paleontologists (pay-lee-on-TAL-uh-jists), scientists who study fossils. Paleontologists are a smart bunch. By knowing about bones, animals, and how they're put together, paleontologists use clues to reconstruct the animal.*

## T. Rex Fossils

All the T. rex clues in the world come from about 30 fossil specimens. Some specimens are nearly complete skeletons, and some are just a few bones, but there are no complete fossils of a T. rex with all of its bones intact. One of the most famous T. rex fossils, named "Sue," includes a delicate bone from the inside of its ear!

## Bones

Most of what we know about T. rex comes from studying fossil bones. But when they're found, the bones aren't assembled into the towering skeletons you see in museums. The skeletons of dead tyrannosauruses often got twisted, stirred, and mixed up as they were buried. Putting them back together is like assembling a puzzle with plenty of pieces missing.

## Muscles

Muscles don't get fossilized, but muscles in living animals are attached to bones. Scientists can tell a lot about T. rex muscles by studying the places on the bones where muscles were attached.

## Footprints

There is only one known T. rex footprint, found in what is now New Mexico. A T. rex's footprint was only a few inches longer than an adult human's footprint, but its feet were three times longer than a human foot.

## Guts

Animals' internal organs hardly ever turn into fossils, so no one knows for sure what a T. rex's innards were like.

## Skin

Fossil impressions of T. rex skin look bumpy, like an alligator's. From fossils, scientists know that some of T. rex's dinosaur relatives had feathers!

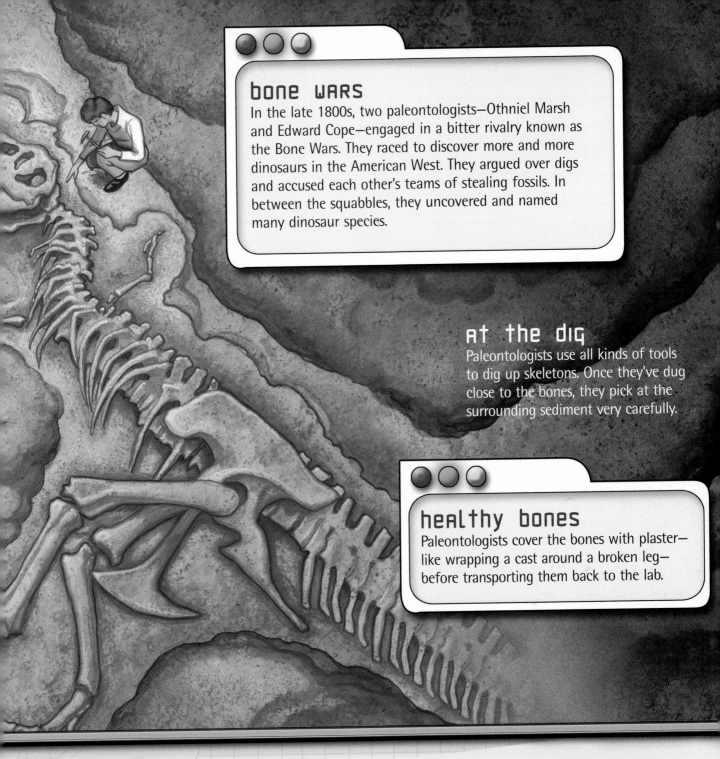

## bone WARS

In the late 1800s, two paleontologists—Othniel Marsh and Edward Cope—engaged in a bitter rivalry known as the Bone Wars. They raced to discover more and more dinosaurs in the American West. They argued over digs and accused each other's teams of stealing fossils. In between the squabbles, they uncovered and named many dinosaur species.

## at the dig

Paleontologists use all kinds of tools to dig up skeletons. Once they've dug close to the bones, they pick at the surrounding sediment very carefully.

## healthy bones

Paleontologists cover the bones with plaster—like wrapping a cast around a broken leg—before transporting them back to the lab.

## Prehistoric Poop

Some paleontologists learn about dinosaurs by studying *coprolites* (KOP-ruh-lites), or fossilized dino dung. A T. rex coprolite found in Saskatchewan, Canada, was almost a foot and a half long and contained bone fragments from an animal the T. rex had eaten.

FOSSILS ARE THE BURIED REMAINS OF ANCIENT PLANTS AND ANIMALS. SOME FOSSILS ARE PRESERVED BONES. OTHERS ARE LIKE MOLDS, IMPRESSIONS LEFT IN SOFT MUD OR SAND THAT LATER TURNED TO STONE. AND SOME ARE STONE THEMSELVES, PLANT AND ANIMAL PARTS REPLACED BY MINERALS AS THEY DECAYED.

# Dino Debates

Because there aren't any living dinosaurs to study, paleontologists have lots to argue about. Here are a couple of debates raging in the scientific world right now.

## Heads and Tails: A Balancing Act

Did T. rex walk with its tail on the ground or held out behind it in the air?

You may have seen old pictures or movies showing a tyrannosaurus standing upright, its tail dragging on the ground. About 30 years ago, scientists began exploring new theories about how dinosaurs stood and walked, but the old idea of the tail-dragging T. rex was popular for a long time.

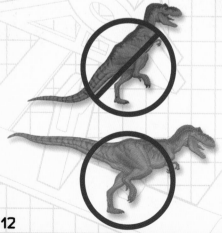

## hot topic

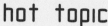

Were T. rex and other dinosaurs *endothermic* (warm-blooded), like mammals and birds, or *ectothermic* (cold-blooded), like reptiles and amphibians?

**Arguments for warm-blooded dinosaurs**

- Dinosaurs were fast, and modern fast-moving animals are endothermic.

- Dinosaurs stood erect, like mammals, instead of sprawling, like reptiles.

- Birds, the modern descendants of dinosaurs, are endothermic.

**Arguments for cold-blooded dinosaurs**

- Dinosaurs were reptiles, and reptiles are ectothermic.

- Dinosaurs like T. rex were really big, and really big, warm-blooded animals have trouble getting rid of heat. So those dinos must have been ectothermic.

- Dinosaur bones and teeth grew in spurts, depending on the warm and cold seasons. That's the way ectothermic animals grow.

## decide for yourself

There isn't a definite answer either way. Dinosaurs may have been endothermic, ectothermic, or something in between. Some may have been warm-blooded while others were cold-blooded. Until more evidence comes along, you're free to pick the theory you like.

It's now believed that T. rex walked stooped over, instead of standing straight. Its tail would have been off the ground. T. rex used its tail for balance. Strong tendons at the base and interlocking bones at the tip helped keep the tail stiff. The dinosaur needed the tail as a counterbalance for its gigantic head.

Was T. rex a hunter . . .

. . . or a scavenger?

## Hunter or Scavenger?

Did T. rex work for its dinner or just eat what it found lying around? Nobody argues about what T. rex ate. With teeth like that, it had to be a meat-eater! Scientists have found fossils with bite marks from tyrannosauruses. And don't forget the bones in the T. rex coprolite!

But at least one famous dinosaur paleontologist thinks that T. rex wasn't a hunter, but a scavenger. Dr. Jack Horner says that T. rex's small eyes, weak arms, and super sense of smell all point to an animal that found its meals by searching for the carcasses of dead dinosaurs.

On the other hand, being a scavenger doesn't mean you can't also be a hunter. Modern lions and hyenas do both. And hunters don't have to have strong arms. Sharks, snakes, and eagles don't have any arms at all!

# Beyond Bones

*One way to learn more about T. rex is to use the science of physics to figure out how its body must have worked.*

## A Mighty Chomp

In 1996, scientists at the University of California at Berkeley did an experiment to find out just how hard a T. rex could bite. The clue was the fossil pelvis, or hip bone, of a triceratops. The pelvis had bite marks left by T. rex teeth, holes almost half an inch deep in the solid bone!

To find out what kind of force was needed to chomp like that, the scientists made a copy of a T. rex tooth out of metal. They put the tooth copy in a hydraulic press that could measure how much force was put on it. Then they took the pelvis of a cow, which is about as hard as the triceratops pelvis, and used the press to make a hole in the bone with the tooth.

The result? The scientists calculated that a tyrannosaurus could bite down with about the same force as an alligator. That's way harder than a lion's bite and way *way* harder than a human's!

**Here's a new word for you:**
BIOMECHANICS (BY-OH-MIH-CAN-IKS). IT'S THE STUDY OF THE ENERGY, FORCES, AND MOTION OF ANIMALS AND HUMANS. IN BIOMECHANICAL EXPERIMENTS, SCIENTISTS MEASURE THINGS LIKE THE STRENGTH OF A T. REX TOOTH, THE FORCE OF AN ALLIGATOR BITE, OR THE ENERGY PRODUCED BY A RUNNING COCKROACH. DISCOVERIES MADE IN THE FIELD OF BIOMECHANICS CAN BE USED IN THE FIELD OF BIOMIMETICS!

# ON YOUR MARKS!

How would T. rex have done in a race against different animals?

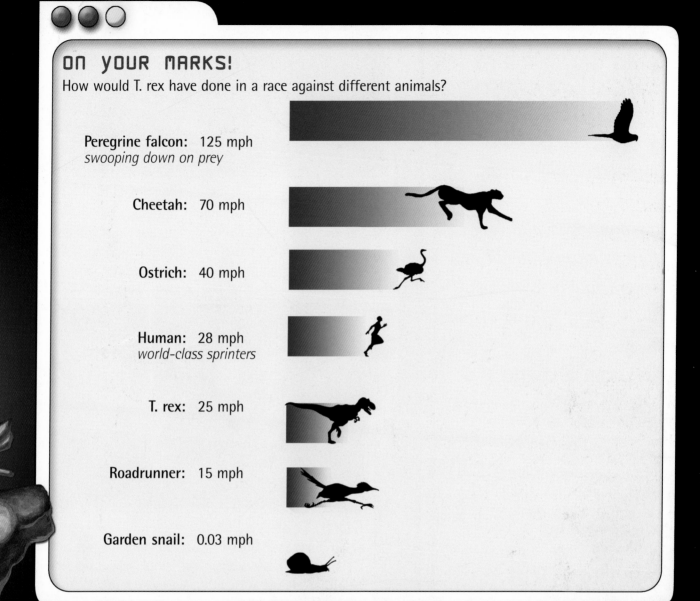

**Peregrine falcon:** 125 mph
*swooping down on prey*

**Cheetah:** 70 mph

**Ostrich:** 40 mph

**Human:** 28 mph
*world-class sprinters*

**T. rex:** 25 mph

**Roadrunner:** 15 mph

**Garden snail:** 0.03 mph

# T. Rex Speed Limit

In another experiment, scientists made a computer model of a T. rex leg to see how big its leg muscles would have needed to be in order to make it run fast. Some paleontologists thought that a T. rex could run as fast as 45 miles per hour. From the computer model, the scientists learned that a T. rex couldn't run nearly that fast, and maybe couldn't run at all! The T. rex speed limit was somewhere between 10 and 25 mph. A T. rex's muscles couldn't have been big enough to move such a big animal any faster.

# Robotic Walkers

*This brings us back to robots. Like your T. rex, a lot of biomimetic robots get around by walking. Different animals walk on different numbers of legs, and the same is true of robots.*

## Six Legs: Scuttle Like an Insect

Six-legged robots have an easier time walking than robots with fewer legs. That's because they have more legs to balance on when they walk. The legs move in two sets of three. Each set is a stable tripod, so while one tripod is moving, the other holds the robot up.

## Four Legs: Trot Like a Horse

Four-legged animals like dogs and horses have different gaits, or ways of walking, depending on how fast they want to go.

### robobug

Most six-legged robots are designed to walk like insects—with a tripod gait. But some insects, such as the American cockroach, can also walk on their two hind legs. Roboticists are working on creating a six-legged robot that can do the same thing.

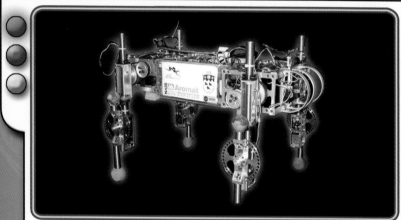

### scout II

Scout II is a four-legged robot that can stand up, sit down, and climb up and down stairs. Knee joints make it possible for Scout II to trot, as well as walk. Scout II can even bound forward on all four legs like an antelope, a gait known as *pronking*. Scout II's designers believe the robot will one day be used for surveillance, bomb disposal, and forestry applications.

## Two Legs: Stroll Like a Human, Strut Like a Bird, Toddle Like a T. Rex

Designers of two-legged robots have a couple of walking styles they can copy from the world of biology. The robot can walk like a human or it can walk like a bird. Those are the only living bipeds. Probably because humans are the ones who build robots, most bipedal robots walk like humans.

There's a good reason to make robots that walk like us: robots of the future will have to work with people. Our houses and workplaces are designed for people to move around in, so a robot would have an easier time if it got around the same way we do.

## ASIMO

ASIMO is a two-legged, humanoid robot from Japan. It has 26 separate motors to control its natural-looking motions. ASIMO can climb stairs, dance, and even play soccer.

knee

ankle

## pigeon-toed

If you watch a bird walk, you'll see that its knees bend the "wrong" way. Birds walk on their toes, like T. rex, and what looks like the bird's knee is actually its ankle.

## Putting Spring in Your Step

Bob Full is a scientist who studies the biomechanics of walking and running animals. By studying the movement patterns of different animals, he discovered that running is like bouncing and walking is like a swinging pendulum. Animals (including people!) store energy in one step and release it in the next. Giving robots springy walking systems can help them walk more like animals.

WALKING ON TWO LEGS IS TOUGH! YOU'VE DONE IT SINCE YOU WERE LITTLE, SO YOU PROBABLY DON'T THINK ABOUT IT. EVERY TIME YOU TAKE A STEP, YOU SPEND SOME TIME WITH ONLY ONE LEG ON THE GROUND. IF A TWO-LEGGED ROBOT GETS JUST A LITTLE OFF-BALANCE, IT CAN TIP OVER.

# Dinobots for Research

*Some dinosaur robots are at the cutting edge of robot research. These experimental dinobots are helping scientists and engineers test out different ways of walking.*

## T. Rex Walking

Scientists at the University of Reading in England are working on a robot they hope will learn to walk like a T. rex, all on its own. The "rexbot" will have two legs for walking and a tail to keep it balanced, just like a real T. rex.

The most important thing about this robot isn't in its legs, but in its brains. The rexbot's computer uses a computer program version of an animal's brain and nervous system. With its neural network program, the robot will figure out, all by itself, how to use its legs and tail to balance and walk.

The walking T. rex robot is an experiment in the branch of computer science called *artificial intelligence*. The goal of artificial intelligence is to build machines that can solve problems, learn, and even think! Artificial intelligence and robotics often go hand in hand, because robot designers would like their robots to work by themselves, without a human controller. To do that, the robots have to be able to navigate and solve problems on their own.

Cog is a robot that uses A.I. to learn. Cog is learning how to move objects and how to get attention, just like a human baby. Cog can find faces, imitate the way people nod and shake their heads, and reach out a hand for objects.

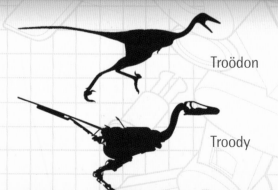

Troödon

Troody

## A.I.

In order to move around and solve problems on their own, advanced robots use artificial intelligence (A.I.) programming. The goal of A.I. is to build intelligent machines.

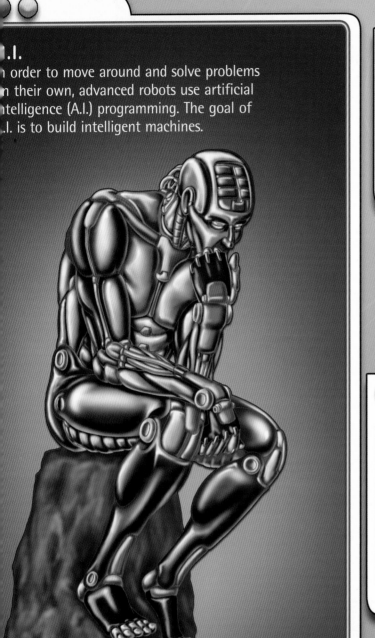

## the declaration of robot independence

Robots that navigate and work by themselves are called autonomous (aw-TAWN-uh-muss) robots.

## intelligence test

How can you tell if a machine is intelligent? The British codebreaker and mathematician Alan Turing suggested this test: Put a machine and a human in another room. Ask them questions in writing. When you get answers (also in writing), can you tell which is the human and which is the machine? If not, the machine is intelligent!

## Troody the Troödon

She's not a tyrannosaurus, but she's a relative. Troody is a robotic Troödon (TROH-o-dawn), a small hunter that lived during the late Cretaceous period, around the same time as T. rex. She looks a little bit like a mechanical chicken. The robotic Troödon has 14 motors in her legs that let her stand up from a sitting position, walk, and sit back down.

Troody was developed by scientists at the Massachusetts Institute of Technology (MIT) Leg Laboratory, a robotics lab that specializes in the creation of walking robots. Troody's inventors have formed their own company and hope to make many different kinds of walking dinosaur robots.

TROODY IS EQUIPPED WITH A VESTIBULAR (VES-TIB-YUH-LER) SYSTEM TO HELP IT BALANCE, SIMILAR TO OUR INNER EARS.

# More Dinobots

*Robot designers of all kinds look to dinosaurs for inspiration. Here are some robotic dinosaurs you might be hearing more about soon.*

## How Many Wrecks Could a T. Rex Wreck if a T. Rex Could Wreck Wrecks?

Plenty, if it's Robosaurus! Is it a T. rex? Well, sort of. The tyrant lizard king is obviously the inspiration for Robosaurus, but this gigantic, car-eating monster is a little more like Godzilla than a real tyrannosaurus. Robosaurus is 40 feet tall. It breathes fire, which no T. rex ever did. When Robosaurus puts on a show, it rolls into the arena, spewing 20-foot flames and stalking its prey, the wily automobile. At the climax of the performance, Robosaurus bends over an unoccupied car, picks it up, and lifts it higher than a five-story building. Then, with a hideous screech of metal, Robosaurus tears the car in half and throws the pieces to the ground!

> ROBOSAURUS, NOT TECHNICALLY A TRUE ROBOT, IS CONTROLLED BY A PILOT SITTING IN THE CAR-EATING MACHINE'S HEAD.

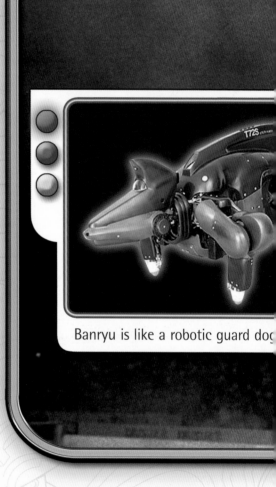

Banryu is like a robotic guard dog

## Four-Legged Guardosaurus

It doesn't walk on two legs, but Banryu is a real, working dinosaur robot! This Japanese robot is about as big as a sheep. Its name means "guard dinosaur" or "guard dragon." The robot is like an alarm system and guard dog rolled into one. It patrols the house, looking and sniffing for intruders or other kinds of trouble. Banryu has a camera and infrared sensor, a sensor to detect changes in temperature, a sonic sensor to listen for noises, and even an odor sensor to sniff for smoke.

If your guard dinosaur detects an intruder, fire, or other danger, it can make noise to alert you, or call you on your cell phone. You can use the phone as a remote control for the robot, take a look at your house with its camera, and even talk to people in the same room as Banryu, using its built-in speaker.

The robot is friendly to its owners and can operate in a "pet mode" as well as guard mode. Banryu isn't just a toy—it's a serious, autonomous robot. You can buy one of your own for about $15,000.

## MAKING IT MOVE

Robosaurus Pilot is a difficult job. By moving his fingers, arms, and feet, the pilot tells Robosaurus what to do. When he lifts his forearm, Robosaurus copies him and raises his mighty, metal forearm too. If the pilot spreads his middle finger and thumb apart, Robosaurus's claw opens. If he brings his middle finger and thumb together, Robosaurus's claw closes. The controller presses on pedals to make Robosaurus turn, speed up, and slow down.

## Why Did the Robot Cross the Road?

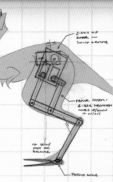

To prove it wasn't chicken! Or was it? Birds are the modern descendants of dinosaurs. In fact, some scientists classify them not as descendants, but as *avian* (birdlike) dinosaurs. When thinking about how dinosaurs might have walked, scientists often compare them to flightless birds such as ostriches and chickens.

Jurassic Chicken is an experimental robot being developed at the University of Florida. The robot will walk on chickenlike legs and feet. This robo-chicken is an artificial intelligence experiment. It will learn to balance and walk on its own. To do that, its legs will be controlled by a neural network, a computer program inspired by the nerve cell connections in the human brain and nervous system.

# Animatronic

# T. Rex

If you go to a natural history museum or science center, you might see an animatronic T. rex. These realistic robot dinosaurs may be the closest people will ever get to seeing a moving, roaring T. rex in the flesh. The creators of animatronic dinosaurs try to make their creatures as accurate as possible, based on the latest scientific theories and fossil discoveries.

### dino breath

The makers of an animatronic T. rex exhibit at the British Museum in London wanted to add extra realism by blowing simulated dinosaur breath around the room.

Knowing that T. rex was a meat-eater, they chose the scent of rotting meat. The stink was so awful, they had to use swamp smells instead!

### flesh of foam

Foam rubber fills out the dinosaur's form.

## Color Patterns

The dinosaur's skin is painted to give it a lifelike color pattern. Artists base the patterns of animatronic dinosaurs on the colors and camouflage patterns of modern animals, but they have a lot of artistic freedom, since no one knows what color a T. rex's skin was!

## Muscles Made of Air

Most animatronic dinosaurs in museums and theme parks are *pneumatic* (noo-MAD-ik), or air-powered. Each "muscle" is a cylinder with a piston inside. A air compressor pushes air into the cylinder to move the piston. (The cylinder is built like a backward bicycle pump, with air coming in and pushing up the handle, instead of the other way around.) Some animatronics use *hydraulic* (hi-DRAW-lik) cylinders powered by oil instead of air.

## silicone skin

Animatronic dinosaurs have skin made of natural or synthetic rubber. The rubber skin's texture is based on fossils of real dinosaur skin.

Only a few fossil imprints of T. rex skin have ever been found. One of them was discovered by Tess Owen, a Canadian girl who was only 12 years old at the time!

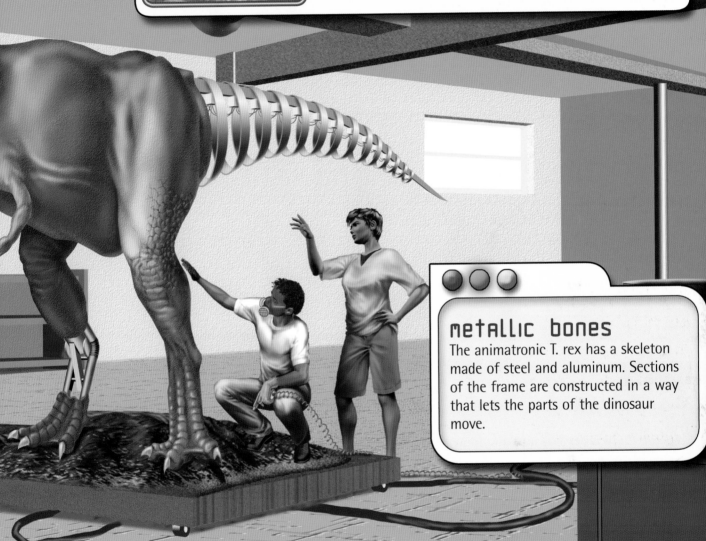

## metallic bones

The animatronic T. rex has a skeleton made of steel and aluminum. Sections of the frame are constructed in a way that lets the parts of the dinosaur move.

## The Brains of the Operation

The dinosaur's movements are controlled by a computer. The computer opens and closes air valves to work the dinosaur's pneumatic muscles. The computer can run different programs to give the dinosaur different movement patterns.

## Stereophonic Animatronic

Recorded roaring and screeching sounds add atmosphere, but just as no one knows what color dinosaurs were, no one knows what sounds they made.

# Action

# Stars

*Animatronic dinosaurs aren't just for museums! They're also stars in movies and at amusement parks.*

## Lights! Cameras! Dinosaurs!

Probably the most famous robot T. rex appeared on-screen in the *Jurassic Park* movies. Movie animatronics are a lot like the ones in museums, but they're often more complicated. A museum T. rex robot usually moves in only a few ways, repeated over and over in a cycle. A movie T. rex robot has to be able to move in many different ways to portray the action in the script. Movie T. rexes are sometimes controlled by a team of puppeteers.

## Coming Soon to a Theme Park Near You

Soon you may see a life-size, walking dinosaur in person. Walt Disney Co. animatronics creators are finishing work on a free-roaming bipedal dinosaur for one of their theme parks in California. It will be controlled from a distance by a human operator.

## Solo Dinobots

A few years ago, two Greek robotics scientists teamed up with an English expert on dinosaur biomechanics to make a dinosaur robot that was completely autonomous. For their dinosaur, they chose an iguanodon, a plant-eater that lived during the early Cretaceous period, about 50 million years earlier than T. rex.

The scientists' robot was eight feet long, half the size of a real iguanodon. Unlike an animatronic dinosaur, it carried its own on-board computer and power supply. The robotic iguanodon could walk around the room, choosing its own path to follow and avoiding things in its way. The scientists hope to build an improved, full-size version with a wide range of realistic actions.

This is what the camera sees—all the operators and puppeteers are out of sight.

Animatronics are controlled with telemetry (tuh-LEM-uh-tree) devices. Some are like the remote controls used with toy cars. These devices can control anything needed for the scene: facial expressions, eye movements, even nostril flares! Some telemetry devices are pieces of equipment worn by puppeteers. When the puppeteers move, their motions are transmitted to the animatronic creature, which then moves in similar ways.

## The Future of Dinobots

Animatronic dinosaurs are OK, but they're stuck in one place. Swinging your head back and forth or pawing the same piece of ground all day can get pretty boring for a machine, and it's not very realistic!

And animatronics operated by people aren't really full-fledged robots, are they? Imagine a future where dinobots are autonomous. They'll be able to walk around all by themselves and interact with people and other robots. But it would probably be a good idea if they didn't try to eat each other!

NOW IT'S TIME FOR YOU TO BUILD YOUR OWN WALKING DINOBOT. TURN THE PAGE AND GET STARTED!

## before you begin

*Take all the parts out of the package and lay them on a flat surface.*
*Read through all of the assembly instructions.*

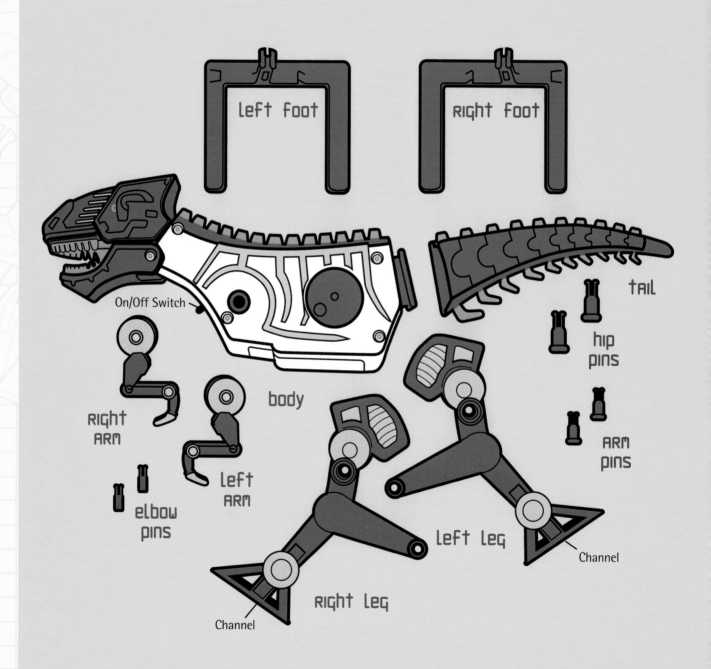

Left foot

Right foot

On/Off Switch

body

tail

hip pins

RIGHT ARM

Left ARM

ARM pins

elbow pins

Left Leg

Channel

RIGHT Leg

Channel

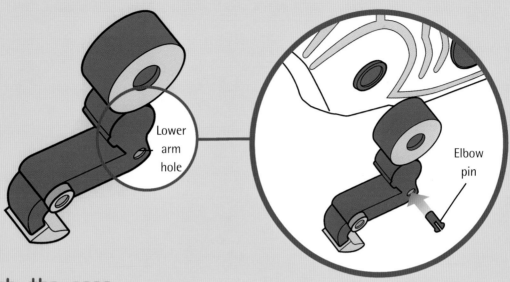

# 1. Attach the Arms

▶ Insert an elbow pin into the lower arm hole of the outside of the left arm. (The left arm is marked "L IN" on the inside.)

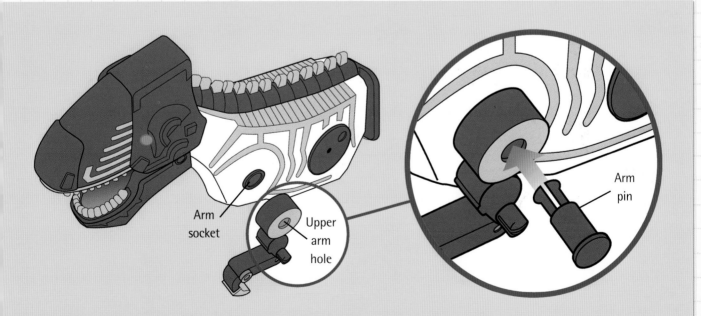

▶ Line up the upper arm hole with the arm socket on the body.

▶ Press an arm pin through the upper arm hole, from the outside of the arm, and into the arm socket, until it snaps into place.

▶ Repeat with the right arm.

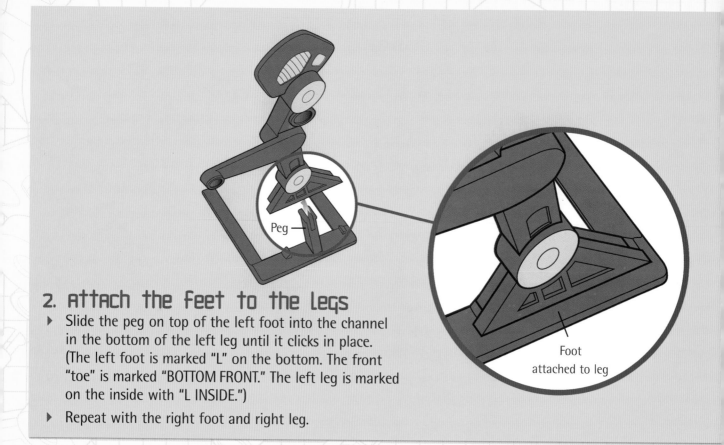

Peg

Foot
attached to leg

## 2. Attach the feet to the legs

▸ Slide the peg on top of the left foot into the channel
in the bottom of the left leg until it clicks in place.
(The left foot is marked "L" on the bottom. The front
"toe" is marked "BOTTOM FRONT." The left leg is marked
on the inside with "L INSIDE.")

▸ Repeat with the right foot and right leg.

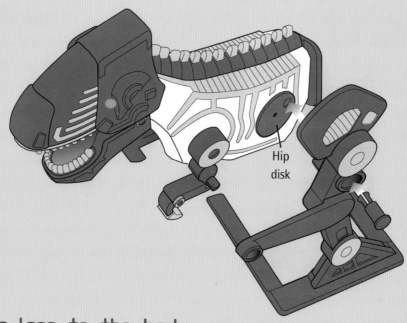

Hip
disk

## 3. Attach the legs to the body

▸ Insert a hip pin through the hole in the left leg.

▸ Press the hip pin into the hole in the left hip
disk until it clicks.

▸ Repeat with the right leg.

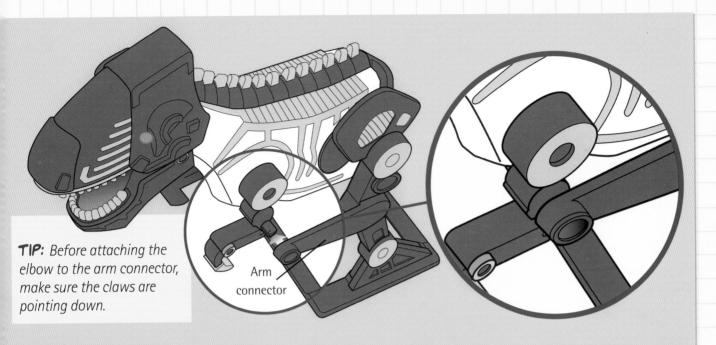

**TIP:** *Before attaching the elbow to the arm connector, make sure the claws are pointing down.*

Arm connector

## 4. connect the arms and legs

▶ Line up the left elbow pin with the hole in the left arm connector and fit the arm connector hole over the pin until it clicks.

▶ Repeat on the right side.

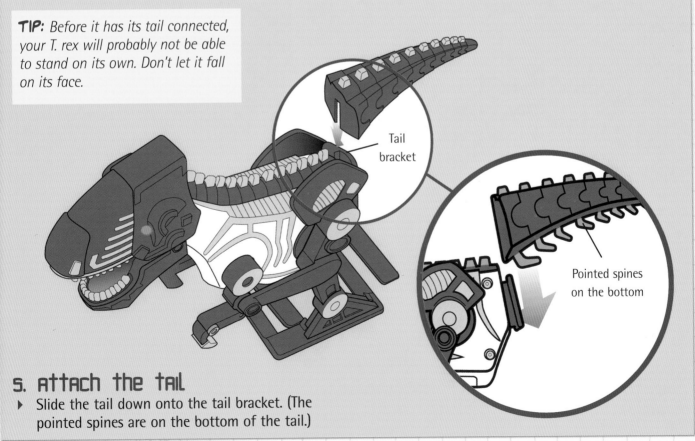

**TIP:** *Before it has its tail connected, your T. rex will probably not be able to stand on its own. Don't let it fall on its face.*

Tail bracket

Pointed spines on the bottom

## 5. attach the tail

▶ Slide the tail down onto the tail bracket. (The pointed spines are on the bottom of the tail.)

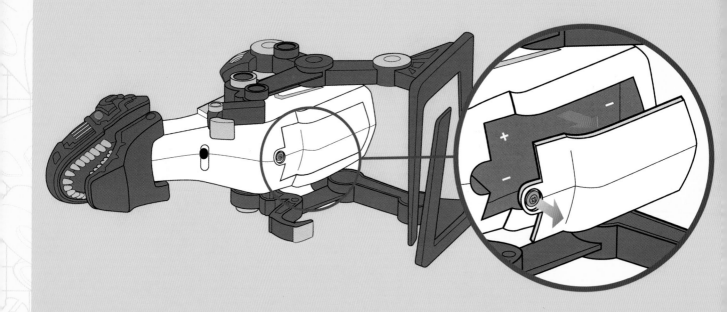

## 6. insert the batteries

▶ Turn the T. rex over and loosen the battery compartment screw.

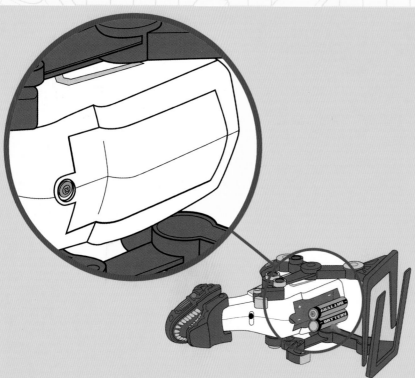

▶ Place two AAA batteries into the battery compartment according to the diagram inside the battery compartment. Screw the battery compartment door back on.

## battery cautions

✔ To ensure proper safety and operation, the battery replacement must always be done by an adult.

✔ Never let a child use this product unless the battery door is secure.

✔ Keep all batteries away from small children, and immediately dispose of any batteries safely.

✔ Batteries are small objects and could be ingested.

✔ Nonrechargeable batteries are not to be recharged.

✔ Rechargeable batteries are to be removed from the toy before being charged.

✔ Rechargeable batteries are only to be charged under adult supervision.

✔ Different types of batteries or new and used batteries are not to be mixed.

✔ Only batteries of the same or equivalent types as recommended are to be used.

✔ Do not mix alkaline, standard (carbon-zinc), or rechargeable (nickel-cadmium) batteries.

✔ Batteries are to be inserted with the correct polarity.

✔ Exhausted batteries are to be removed from the toy.

✔ The supply terminals are not to be short-circuited.

## 7. turn it on!

▸ Set the T. rex on its feet and slide the ON/OFF switch (on the T. rex's throat) to ON.

## troubleshooting

If you've followed these assembly instructions and your T. rex doesn't work when you switch it on, follow these tips:

*If your T. rex trips on its own feet:*

▸ Make sure all the pins are inserted all the way.

*If your T. rex doesn't walk properly or falls down:*

▸ Make sure the T. rex's "claws" point down (see step 4).

*If your T. rex doesn't walk at all or the lights don't come on:*

▸ Make sure the batteries are inserted correctly.

▸ Make sure the batteries are fresh.

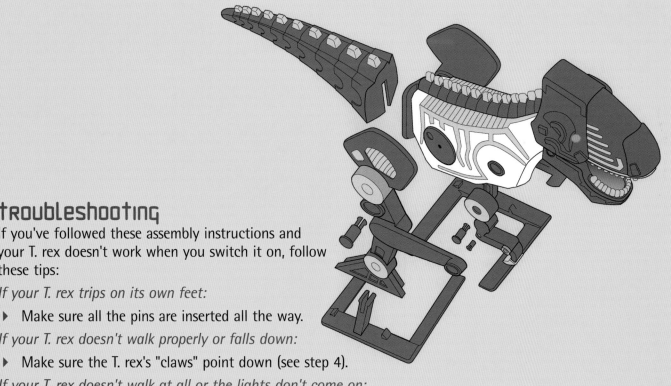

# Robotic T. Rex Experiments

*You've learned about T. rex and the robots that resemble it. You've constructed a robotic T. rex of your own. Now you're ready to experiment and see what your T. rex can do.*

## Tale of the Tail

What happens if you remove your T. rex's tail? When you switch it on and set it down, can it walk? What's the farthest it can walk with no tail? Can it take two tail-free steps before doing a nosedive? The way your T. rex performs (or doesn't perform) without a tail can give you insight into the real T. rex and how it relied on its tail for balance.

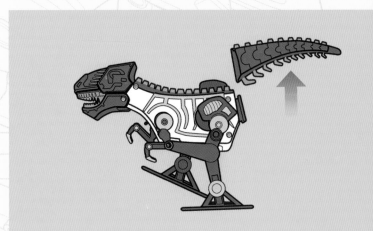

## Push and Pull

How much push-power does your T. rex have? Can it knock over small objects like paperback books? Can it budge objects along the floor or across a tabletop? Your T. rex might turn aside when it bumps up against an obstacle—can you construct something it can push without turning? Maybe it pulls better than it pushes. Connect objects to its tail with string or a piece of tape. Switch it on and see how well it performs. How heavy do the objects have to be before the clutch slips and clicks?

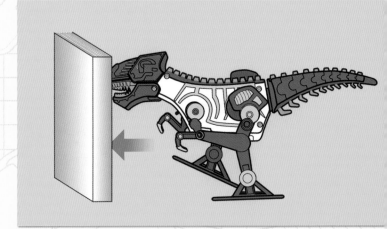

## Uphill Battle

Set your T. rex on a tilted surface—like a baking sheet—switch it on, and watch it climb. How steep can the surface be before the T. rex just can't keep climbing? How steep does it have to be before the T. rex slips back down to the bottom? Do you think your T. rex can walk downhill as well as it walks uphill? Try it and find out.

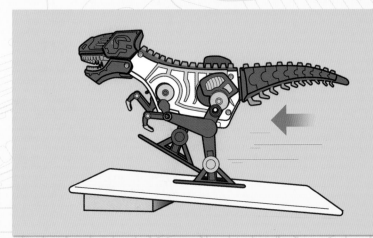